TO SEE THE MOON

by Ethel Bacon
illustrated by David Ray

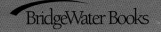
BridgeWater Books

Published by BridgeWater Books, an imprint and registered trademark of
Troll Communications L.L.C.

Printed in the United States of America.
10 9 8 7 6 5 4 3 2 1

Library of Congress Cataloging-in-Publication Data
Bacon, Ethel.
To see the moon / by Ethel Bacon; pictures by David Ray.
p.   cm.
Summary: Despite everyone's doubts, Diane determines that her puppy,
the smallest and weakest in the sled dog litter, will grow strong
and participate in the one-dog race twelve months away.
ISBN 0-8167-3822-X
[1. Dogs—Fiction. 2. Sled dogs—Fiction.] I. Ray, David, ill.
II. Title.
PZ7.B1325To   1996
[Fic]—dc20   95-8070

For all of my nieces and nephews, with love. —E.B.

To MaryAnne Dumont and Boo. —D.R.

Puffy winter clouds dropped new snow onto the faraway mountains as a little girl ran down a frozen dirt road. Her name was Diane and she was on the way to her neighbor's sled dog kennel. Alongside the road a brook gurgled under its cover of gray ice. Through bare branches Diane saw the snow on the mountaintops and thought, I am going to get my very own sled dog. *Hoo-hoo.* In the cold December air her breath swirled white as the new moon hanging in the western sky.

Eight puppies rushed toward her, tumbling and biting one another. The smallest one crawled underneath the others and chewed her shoelaces. She picked him up.

"You want him?" the neighbor asked. "You can have him."

He was the littlest one, but he had chosen Diane.

"Never be much of a sled dog," her older brother said when Diane brought the puppy home.

On the night of the full moon in January, Diane walked to the house of her friend the old farmer with the puppy snuggled in her jacket.

"Where are you going with the wee doggie?" he asked.

"Going up the hill to see the moon," Diane told him. He watched as she went out of the warm kitchen, past the old apple tree, across the meadow, through his spruce woods to the windy hilltop.

Far down in the kennel the sled dogs howled at the full moon, the Wolf Moon. The tiny puppy shivered.

On this night of the Wolf Moon in January, Diane told her little puppy, "You will grow strong, my very own Eskimo dog. Your name will be Kimo."

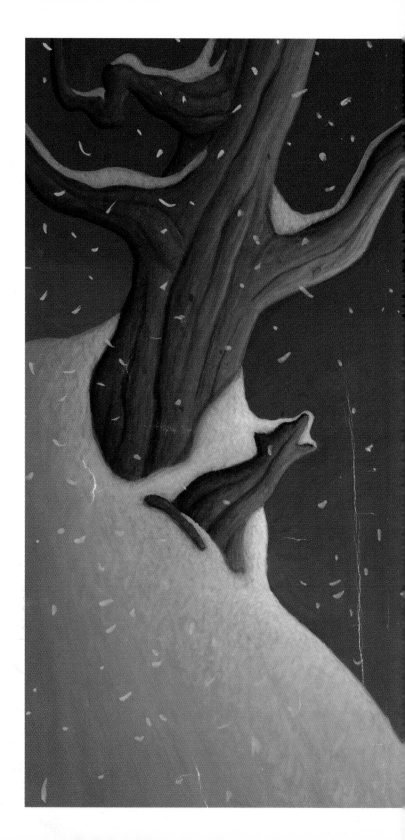

Kimo followed Diane through the snow in February. He sat in her footprints to rest while she waited for him on the windy hilltop. The Snow Moon looked down on the cold winter world. Dry grasses rustled in the night wind.

"Listen," she whispered.

Kimo sat close and looked up into her eyes.

In March the old farmer boiled maple syrup day and night. Steam from his sugarhouse rose up into the light of the Sugar Moon.

Kimo wore a blue collar and walked on a leash. Diane's brother laughed to see her teaching him sled dog commands.

"Kimo, gee!" They turned to the right.

"Kimo, haw!" They turned to the left.

When Kimo finally understood what she meant, he was a happy dog. They raced between two maple trees.

"Straight ahead! Straight ahead!" Diane shouted.

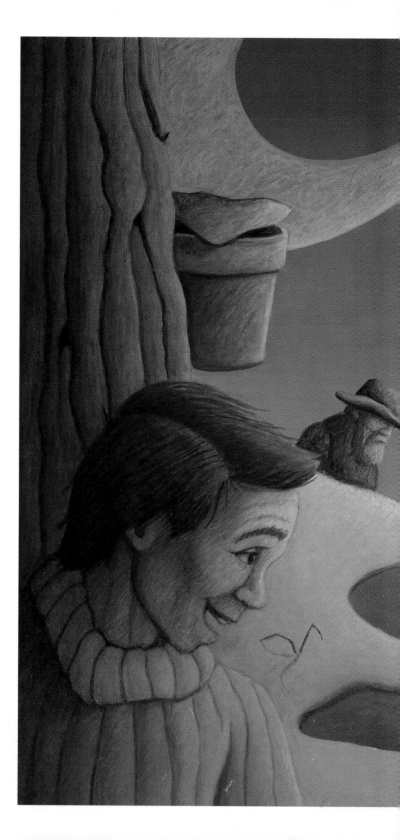

Spring peepers peeped a mighty chorus in April. The Grass Moon came up across the valley. Kimo ran big circles in the meadow, sniffing the new grass. Then he raced to Diane and tumbled onto her feet.

In May the Planter's Moon shone bright behind tiny green leaves. Kimo was five months old. Diane slipped a racing harness over his head and front legs. Holding the harness, she stamped her feet on the ground, saying, "Kimo, hike." He ran sideways, looking at her.

"He'll never win a race!" her brother sighed.

One day when Diane put the harness over Kimo's head, he quickly pushed his front legs into it. She held on and called out, "Kimo, hike!" He flew across the spring beauties that covered the floor of the woods like beautiful snow. Diane cheered, "Good boy, good boy!"

When Diane ran with Kimo in June, perfume of apple blossoms floated in the air, fireflies danced above white daisies, and the Flower Moon rolled across the sky.

Red clover and buttercups painted the roadside in July. Grasses grew tall and sweet. The farmer cut hay, the month of the Hay Moon. Kimo pounced on grasshoppers in the meadow until he was tired out. Then Diane harnessed him and sat on her bicycle, holding the leash. Kimo walked ahead of her as she pedaled slowly along the dirt road.

In August corn stood tall, with long, shiny leaves whispering in every puff of hot summer breeze. Diane and Kimo sat on the hilltop, the red sun sinking behind them, the Maize Moon, big and pink, rising in front of them.

To help the farmer, Diane hitched Kimo to a wagon in September. They pulled heavy loads of pumpkins. The Harvest Moon came up in the east before they finished, while the sky in the west was peach and blue.

Each day Diane harnessed Kimo, then told him, "Okay, let's go!" Now he ran so fast that she sat on her bicycle without pedaling. "Easy!" she cried as she put on the brakes, skidding around a corner. One night she dreamed of a sled dog race. Kimo was running.

When the orange moon came up in October, Diane and Kimo watched a fox leap high, twisting like a fish, to toss a mouse in the air. Then fox nose followed mouse tail along the ground. It was the night of the Hunter's Moon.

Kimo was ten months old. Diane borrowed a sled dog rig with three wheels. Kimo ducked his head into his harness, shoved his front legs in, and stood waiting for his command.

"Kimo, hike!" Diane gave a push and he raced off. The noisy rig did not frighten him. He just wanted to run and to pull. Diane stood on the platform like a chariot driver.

In November thin blankets of frost were spread each night. Kimo pulled Diane on frozen dirt roads while the Frost Moon sailed high above them.

Afternoons darkened, nights were long in December. Snow clouds rolled down from distant hills. When Diane stood on the dogsled runners for the first time, she knew she would sign up for the one-dog race.

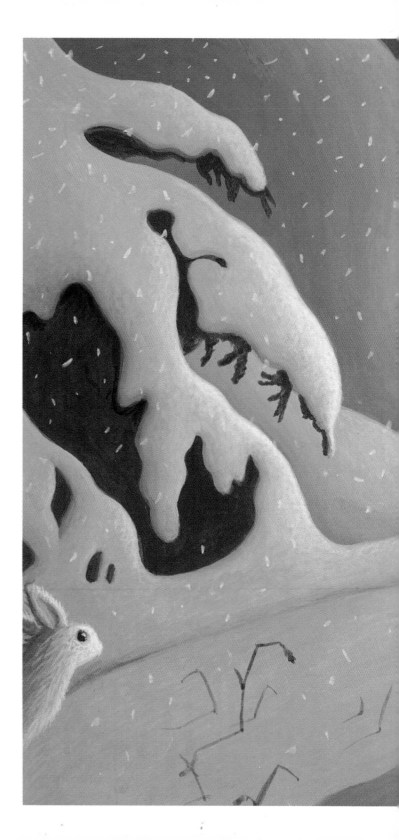

The race started early on a cold, clear day. Seven children had signed up to be mushers. They walked out to the starting line holding their nervous dogs, dragging their dogsleds. Crowds of people stood talking and waiting.

One by one the young mushers left the starting line. The first dog ran zigzag all the way, looking at the people. The next dog started out, then turned around and ran back. One dog stopped to say hello to everyone, even though his master kept shouting, "Okay, let's go!"

Finally it was Diane's turn. She bent down to Kimo and whispered, "Run fast." She kissed the top of his head and hurried to the sled handle.

"Five! Four! Three! Two! One! Go!" The starter's flag snapped down.

Diane screamed, "Kimo, hike!" He ran sideways, looking back at her.

"Straight ahead! Straight ahead!" she shouted.

And Kimo poured all of his excitement and energy into that command. Faster and faster the sled clattered over the hard-packed snow. People leaned over to see who was coming.

"Look at that little one go!" someone said.

Diane hung on, struggling to keep her feet on the narrow runners. Her brother grabbed for Kimo's harness at the finish line.

"Whoa, you ran a good race," he said.

"Did you see us? Did you see us?" Diane threw her arms around Kimo's neck. They had won the race.

The night of the full moon that December, the Longest Night Moon, Diane and Kimo went to the farmer's house to show him their blue ribbon.

"You have a good little sled dog," he said.

Then they went out of the warm kitchen, past the old apple tree, across the meadow, into his silent spruce woods, where the moon hung in the branches like a silver ball. On the windy hilltop Kimo sat close beside Diane.

That night, as the moon floated in the dark blue sky, Diane dreamed of a sled dog team. Kimo was the leader.